DOOMED WITHOUT DAVE DANZIG . . .

"Sure, you guys have won the March Madness contest," Jim said. "Congratulations. But you want to watch first place go down the tubes? Then just keep playing the way you played today."

Derek was waiting for him to say more, but Jim just grabbed his clipboard, the mesh ball bag, and his blue-and-white Branford varsity jacket. Then he headed for the exit.

Nate shrugged. "I've got nothing to add."

As the Bulls slowly followed their coaches, Will mumbled to Derek, "Mark and Jo played a good game, but there's nobody like Dave at the point. I don't know what we're going to do without him."

Derek nodded. With Dave missing, the whole team was out of sync.

If we don't find a way to get Mrs. Danzig to lift Dave's grounding, Derek thought, *the Bulls are going to self-destruct!*

ABOVE THE RIM

by
Hank Herman

BANTAM BOOKS
NEW YORK · TORONTO · LONDON · SYDNEY · AUCKLAND

RL 2.6, 007-010

ABOVE THE RIM

A Bantam Book / May 1997

Produced by Daniel Weiss Associates, Inc.
33 West 17th Street
New York, NY 10011.

Cover art by Jeff Mangiat.

All rights reserved.

ISBN: 0-553-48474-5
Published simultaneously in the United States and Canada

Bantam Books are published by Bantam Books; a division of Bantam
Doubleday Dell Publishing Group, Inc. Its trademark, consisting of the
words "Bantam Books" and the portrayal of a rooster, is Registered in U.S.
Patent and Trademark Office and in other countries. Marca Registrada.
Bantam Books, 1540 Broadway, New York, New York 10036.

PRINTED IN THE UNITED STATES OF AMERICA

OPM   0 9 8 7 6 5 4 3 2 1

To Aunt Sandy

Will Hopwood skidded on a patch of ice as he tried to dribble on the Jefferson Park blacktop.

"Man!" Derek Roberts heard Will mutter. "As if this game weren't hard *enough*."

Derek could see what Will was trying to do: back his way in closer to the hoop. At five foot four, Will was the tallest member of the Branford Bulls, a team of basketball-crazy fifth graders. And he was strong too.

But Will's defender was stronger. Blocking his path to the hoop was his

1

older brother, Jim, co-captain of the Branford High varsity basketball team and one of two teenage coaches of the Bulls.

Even though Derek was on the same scrimmage team as Will—the Bulls' starters were playing against the subs and coaches—he had to laugh at the look of frustration on Will's face. He knew Will was *dying* to score against his older brother.

In your dreams, Derek thought. Although Nate Bowman, the Bulls' other teenage coach, sometimes went easy when he played against the younger kids, Jim always went all out. Especially against his little brother.

About ten feet from the basket Will wasn't able to back Jim in any farther. Will leaped, turned in the air to face the hoop, and fired. Normally his turn-around jumper was a sure bet. But this time he was forced to shoot higher because of Jim's outstretched hand.

The shot thudded off the back of the rim and bounced way up in the air.

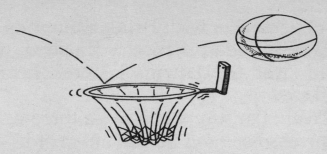

As Derek crashed the boards going after the rebound, he caught a glimpse of Will standing flat-footed, as if he were glued to the blacktop from where he'd taken the shot. Derek knew Will was about to get in trouble.

"Will!" Jim exploded. "What are you doing, sight-seeing? Don't just stand there—follow your shot!"

Guess I know my coaches, Derek chuckled to himself. Jim hated it when the Bulls screwed up on fundamentals. Boxing out on rebounds, setting picks to free your teammates, following your own shots—these were the kind of things Jim emphasized again and again and *again.*

To Derek's amazement, however, Will paid no attention to his brother's scolding. Instead, he was involved in a conversation with Brian Simmons.

"The *minute* practice is finished, we head over to Danzig's," Derek heard Will say.

"Yeah, I'm sure while we're there we'll think of *something*," Brian answered.

Oh, that's great! Derek thought sarcastically. *They're talking about Dave and Mrs. Danzig again. We've got an important game against the Essex Eagles in two days, and all anyone can concentrate on is Dave's being grounded!*

Just a week earlier the Bulls had beaten the tough Portsmouth Panthers to take sole possession of first place in the Danville County Basketball League. And the team that was on top as of March first would win top prize in the league's March Madness contest: an unbelievable, deluxe trip to the NCAA Final Four in Indianapolis!

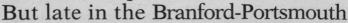

But late in the Branford-Portsmouth

game, David Danzig, the Bulls' long-haired, short-tempered point guard, had blown up . . . *again*. And *this* time his mother had laid down the law: Dave was grounded for a month. The punishment covered the Bulls' next three regular-season games, which would have been bad enough. But the NCAA championships were also coming up. So on top of missing his own games, now Dave wouldn't be able to go with the Bulls on their amazing trip to Indianapolis!

That had been the previous Saturday. Now it was Thursday—and the Bulls had talked about nothing but Dave's grounding since.

Derek had come down with the rebound and whipped the ball out to Jo on the perimeter to start the play over. He saw Jim glaring at Will and Brian.

"What are you two gabbing about?" Jim demanded, grabbing the ball from Jo.

Brian and Will looked at each other. "We were just, uh—," Brian mumbled, running his hand nervously over his fade haircut.

"Yeah, *I* know," Jim cut him off. "You were just talking about Dave again. Well, I've got news for you. The way you guys have been practicing all week, you could *lose* to the Eagles!"

Derek knew that Jim was right. The Eagles were one of the worst teams in the league, but the Bulls had an unfortunate habit of taking the weak teams lightly and playing down to their level. Just the week before the Portsmouth game, the Bulls had managed to find a way to lose to the lowly Winsted Wildcats.

Besides, the Eagles had Sky Jones. Jones was the kind of player who could single-handedly take over a game. He and Derek were in a class by themselves.

Though Derek would never *dream* of saying it to anyone, there were certain things that were just *accepted* around Branford. And one of them was that Sky Jones and Derek Roberts, son of former

NBA great Harold "Rebound" Roberts, were the top two players in the league. Those two, plus Will Hopwood, were locks to make the Danville County Basketball League All-Star team, which would be announced in just a few weeks.

As Derek waited for Jim to stop talk- ing, he adjusted the red-white-and-blue wristbands he always wore. *Guess I don't*  *have to worry about sweating too much in this weather,* he thought. He noticed that MJ Jordan, one of the subs, was actually playing with gloves on! Derek laughed. *Hardly matters, the way* he *shoots!*

Derek found himself thinking for about the hundredth time that it was definitely no picnic playing hoops outdoors in Branford, Illinois, in early March. But the Jefferson Park playground was their only choice. There was simply no indoor court available to the Bulls in Branford.

Jim finally handed the ball back to Jo, saying, "Okay, let's get started again. And *this* time everyone focus on the game—not on Dave Danzig."

Jo dribbled at the top of the key. The only female starter in the league, she was an awesome ball handler and passer, and she always spotted the open man. Derek, standing to the right of the foul line, sensed he'd get the ball quickly.

Sure enough, as Derek sliced toward the hoop, Jo hit him with a perfect bounce pass. Derek thought he had a clear path to the basket. But then Nate Bowman, his defender, planted his huge body in front of him.

Rather than charge into the rock-solid teenager, Derek wisely kicked the ball back out to Mark Fisher, who was waiting on the perimeter. But though the pass was perfect, the ball hit Mark right in the face.

To Derek's horror, Mark staggered, then slumped over onto the cold blacktop. All movement stopped. The Bulls fell silent.

Oh, man, I must have thrown that ball too hard, Derek thought. He felt a queasy sensation in the pit of his stomach. Then he detected the first hint of a smile on Mark's face, and he knew that Mark wasn't really hurt. The Bulls' sixth man, now in the starting lineup because of Dave's absence, was just goofing around, as usual.

Mark suddenly sat up straight, a wise-guy grin on his face. "Just wanted to show you I could use my head," he quipped.

Jim reached down to pull Mark up off the ground. "Come on, you lamebrain," the annoyed coach said. "It's barely thirty degrees, and you're sitting on the frozen ground. What are you thinking?"

"*I* can't help it if Derek passes too hard," Mark complained, fumbling for an excuse.

"Derek's pass was perfect," Jim said impatiently. "You were just out to lunch—like the rest of the team today."

As Jim talked he got more and more worked up, and his voice got louder. Derek had noticed that this seemed to happen to him often.

"You know, you guys never learn," Jim went on. He was now facing the entire team, not just Mark, and he was pounding the ball on the blacktop impatiently. "Two weeks ago you lost to the pathetic Winsted Wildcats. . . ."

Some of the Bulls stared at the bare trees surrounding the blacktop. Most of them looked down at their shoes. Derek knew that once Jim got going, he could talk for a while.

"Then last week you managed to beat Portsmouth," Jim continued, "but it took a last-minute miracle from *this* yo-yo"—he put his hand on Mark's head—"to save you. Now, on Saturday we'll be playing without Danzig, and you guys *still* seem to think you've got the game against Essex all wrapped up!"

His lecture was followed by a short silence.

"Coach's right," Derek said softly. For Derek, those two words almost amounted to a *speech*.

Normally when Derek spoke, the Bulls listened. But not this time.

"We're not worried about the Eagles," Chunky Schwartz called out. Derek was surprised by his outburst. Chunky, the Bulls' wide-bodied backup center, was usually the least confident kid on the team.

"Eagles, shmeagles," Mark added. "We've got more important things to worry about."

Jim folded his arms across his chest. "Like?" he asked.

"Like finding a way to get Mrs. Danzig to lift Dave's grounding before our trip to Indianapolis," Mark answered. *"Duh,"* he added, as if he thought what he'd said was pretty obvious.

All of a sudden Derek saw Brian's dark eyes light up. He looked excited. "Hey," Brian cried out, "I've got a really great idea!"

Derek winced.

Earlier in the week the Bulls had tried two of Brian's "really great ideas" for getting Dave off the hook—and had gotten absolutely nowhere. *If we follow any more of Brian's wild ideas,* Derek worried, *Mrs. Danzig is liable to* extend *Dave's grounding rather than* lift *it!*

CHAPTER 2

"Come on, guys," Brian urged, "we gotta hurry. We need to be there before Mrs. Danzig gets home from work."

As soon as Jim had given up on trying to get the Bulls to practice, Brian had hustled them out the front gates of Jefferson Park. Now they were half walking, half running down Mulberry Avenue in the direction of the Danzig house. Derek was kind of surprised that the team was even following Brian, since both his earlier schemes had failed. But when Brian got an idea in his head, it was just about impossible to stop him from seeing it through.

Derek loved the sound of their sneakers crunching on the snow as the Bulls made their way down the avenue toward McVey Street, where the Danzigs and the Simmonses lived. Dave and Brian were actually next-door neighbors—something that Derek envied a lot. He wished he had a best friend living next door.

Will nudged Brian's arm. "I'm not going along with another of your so-called brilliant plans unless I hear about it first," he said as they trudged along.

"Yeah, I hope this great idea of yours works better than your inspiration about giving her flowers," Mark piped up. Mark had the hood of his big blue parka pulled over his head, and Derek could see his breath in front of his face as he spoke. "That cost us three bucks each—and look how far it got us!"

"Just about as far as washing her car, Brian's other brainstorm," Jo added, adjusting her green baseball cap, which she wore backward, as usual. "I nearly got frostbite trying to soap up that car in this weather—and Mrs. D. *still* wouldn't lift Dave's grounding."

"Just wait," Brian assured them with a smug smile.

For a guy with such harebrained ideas, Derek thought, *he's sure got a lot of confidence.*

When they got to number twenty-seven McVey Street, Brian bolted up the front steps and let himself in without even knocking. The rest of the Bulls followed. Derek could hear the TV on in the living room.

Dave was sprawled on the couch opposite the TV, legs over the armrest, books and papers spread out in front of him.

"What are you doing?" Mark asked.

"What does it *look* like I'm doing, genius?" Dave replied, shaking his long blond hair out of his face. "I'm doing homework. You know, it wasn't just going ballistic with Air Ball Archibald in the Portsmouth game that got me grounded. That D I got on the *Old Yeller* test didn't thrill my mom too much either. Gotta pick up those grades."

"Speaking of your mom," Brian cut in, "she's not home yet, is she?"

"No. Why?" Dave asked.

"Because I've got another great idea to get you ungrounded!" Brian answered. His hands flew all over the place as he talked.

Dave looked at Brian warily. "*Another* great idea? Wasn't the first one—*and* the second one—supposed to guarantee I'd be ungrounded?"

Derek laughed. Obviously Dave thought Brian's ideas were about as lame as the rest of the Bulls did.

"Make fun if you want," Brian went on, "but this one's foolproof. You tell me: What woman can resist the charm of a gourmet candlelit meal?"

"Yeah?" Will challenged. "Where are we gonna get the bucks to take Mrs. Danzig out to a fancy restaurant?"

"We're *not* taking her out," Brian

replied, his dark eyes sparkling. "We're *cooking*."

Derek could not believe what they'd done to the Danzigs' kitchen.

Dave had told the Bulls he expected his mom home by a quarter to six. That had given them all of  forty-five minutes to prepare Brian's "gourmet" meal. In the mad rush, two plates had been smashed to smithereens, and three eggs had crashed to the floor, splattering yellow goo all over the white tiles and the lower part of the wall. Discarded paper towels, aluminum foil, and plastic wrap were scattered everywhere.

The one detail Brian had neglected, Derek now realized, was a cleanup crew.

"Let's see . . . ," Brian said, the tip of a pen in his mouth as he thought. Brian was hand-lettering the menu for the evening's meal. "What do you think we ought to call Mark's hamburger concoction?"

"Sudden Death?" Jo offered.

"How about a Big Mark?" Will suggested.

"That's it!" Brian exclaimed, snapping his fingers. "And I want to give the scrambled eggs I made a fancy, French-sounding name. . . ."

"Eggs *Bri-an?*" MJ Jordan suggested, giving the *Bri-an* his best French accent.

"That's it!" Brian said enthusiastically. "You guys are good!"

Brian carefully wrote "Big Mark" and "Eggs *Bri-an*" on a piece of cardboard Dave had scavenged from his mother's bureau. Then he added "Chunky's Cheddar" for the cheese Chunky had chopped up into little cubes for an appetizer.

As Brian filled out the menu, his mouth turned down at the corners. "Hmmm," he said. "It's five-thirty-five already, and we don't have a dessert yet."

Derek opened the door to the pantry and took out a Hershey's bar. He held it up for Brian to see. He was kidding—but Brian took him seriously.

"Perfect!" Brian said as Derek shook his head. He watched Brian take the candy bar out of its wrapper, break it up into little squares, and put it into a fancy-looking glass bowl.

"We'll call it Chocolate Suicide," Brian declared. He took a final look at the table. "Great," he concluded, "that gives us a four-course meal."

Derek wasn't sure how appetizing Mrs. Danzig would find the Big Mark or the Eggs *Bri-an,* but he had to admit one thing: The Bulls, under Brian's supervision, had done a pretty good job with the dining room.

Jo had located a blue linen tablecloth and white linen napkins in a cabinet over the sink in the kitchen, and Dave had found two unused long white candles, which he placed in brass candlesticks on the dining room table. When Brian laid out the napkins and the silver, the table didn't look half bad.

As a finishing touch, Brian used a marking pen to draw a fake mustache on himself.

At the sound of Mrs. Danzig's car pulling into the driveway, Brian commanded the Bulls to take their positions. He would greet her at the door. Chunky would take care of the seating. The rest of the Bulls were to hover around the table, ready to satisfy any request.

"And Mark," he added, *"whatever you do, don't let her into the kitchen!"*

Brian met Mrs. Danzig at the front door with a bow. "Table for one, madame?" he asked as suavely as he could. Dave smiled nervously as he lit the candles on the table.

Derek was always impressed by how pretty Dave's mother was. She had blond hair and big blue eyes—just like Dave. She always dressed nicely. And she still looked fresh after a long day at work.

He had a hard time reading Mrs. Danzig's expression. Obviously Brian's greeting had tipped her off that something was up, but she looked as though she was willing to play along with it.

With laughter in her eyes, she looked right at her son. "All right, what are you boys trying to pull *this* time?"

Before Dave could answer, Brian stepped in. "Just a candlelit gourmet dinner for our favorite mom who's worked hard all day long."

Mrs. Danzig rolled her eyes. But curiosity propelled her toward the dining room table.

Chunky pulled out a chair for her. "Allow me," he said. "And let me suggest Chunky's Cheddar to start. I prepared it myself."

Mrs. Danzig took a chunk of cheese with her fork. "Mmm," she said in a tone of exaggerated ecstasy. "It *is* delicious."

Dave's mother moved on to her Big Mark and then the Eggs *Bri-an*. She seemed to be enjoying the meal. Brian hovered over her, offering her soda, then coffee. Derek could tell by Brian's pleased expression that he thought he'd finally hit on something to win Mrs. D. over.

Derek, however, wasn't so sure.

Finally Mrs. Danzig primly patted her mouth with the white cloth napkin. "I think I'll pass on the Chocolate Suicide," she said. "I'm not used to such a delicious, filling meal."

"I hope everything has been to your satisfaction, madame?" Brian asked expectantly.

"Oh, yes indeed," Mrs. Danzig replied. "My compliments to the chef." She looked around at all the Bulls. "And to your whole staff."

Brian beamed.

Dave waited silently, a hopeful look on his face.

"But," Mrs. Danzig continued, "Dave's grounding is still in effect."

Hearing her words, Chunky dropped the silverware he had just cleared from the table. Brian's smile froze on his face. Dave groaned. The rest of the Bulls looked as though they'd just lost a big game on a buzzer-beater from mid-court.

I knew it! Derek thought. *I just knew it! It's going to take a lot more than sending her flowers, washing her car, and making her a candlelit dinner to change Mrs. Danzig's mind.*

The question, Derek wondered, was *What?*

CHAPTER 3

Derek knew he wasn't supposed to leave his feet playing defense; his father had drilled him on that at least a hundred times. But what was he supposed to do? At five foot two, Derek was the second-tallest player on the Bulls after Will. But his dad, Harold "Rebound" Roberts, was just under seven feet tall.

This, Derek thought with a chuckle, *is what the TV announcers would call a mismatch!*

Mr. Roberts dribbled the ball on the rough, recently shoveled surface of the driveway, his back to the basket.

Derek desperately used his body to try to keep his father out of shooting range, but his defense was kind of hopeless. Though Mr. Roberts usually kept their one-on-one games fairly close, Derek knew his dad, a Hall of Famer, could score pretty much whenever he wanted. He didn't wear two NBA championship rings on his hand for nothing.

About eight feet from the basket Harold Roberts peeked over his left shoulder, then wheeled and sent up a feathery sky hook. The ball gently swished through the hoop, snapping the net back. It was a shot Derek had seen on countless highlight clips of his father's games.

"Cool, Dad," Derek teased, "but why don't you play me *facing* the basket so you can't use your height advantage so much? And how 'bout taking a *real* shot? Nobody takes hook shots anymore."

"And it's a crying shame," Mr. Roberts responded in his deep voice. "The hook shot is one of the most effective shots around. It's just about impossible to defend against. But you young hot dogs don't use it because it doesn't *look* good. All kids want to do today is dribble between their legs, work on their spin moves, and throw no-look passes. When I was in the NBA—"

"When you were in the NBA," Derek interrupted, "dinosaurs still roamed the earth."

Beneath his dad's mustache, Derek could see that he was smiling. Mr. Roberts had taught his son to be respectful, but Derek knew his father had a sense of humor—and Derek knew what he could get away with.

They both laughed.

"Hey, what time is it?" Derek asked in alarm. He was worried they'd gotten so caught up in their one-on-one match that they'd played beyond their planned departure time for the Bulls' game in Essex.

"Calm down, son. We've still got a few minutes," Mr. Roberts reassured him. "By the way," he continued as he checked the ball for Derek, "what's the latest between Dave and his mom on that grounding business? That get worked out yet?"

Derek, sensing his father had let his guard down, drove quickly to his right. Mr. Roberts was caught flat-footed, and Derek scored an easy layup.

"Schooled you that time," Derek couldn't resist saying. When his father didn't respond but just smiled, Derek became suspicious—and a little upset. "You didn't *let* me score, did you?"

"No, I didn't *let* you score, son," the huge man said, placing a large, meaty hand on Derek's shoulder. "You've gotten too big and too good for that. I'm just not quite as quick as I was in my playing days."

Derek saw a faraway look on his father's face. *Man,* Derek thought, *my dad sure must miss being an NBA star.*

Mr. Roberts snapped out of it. "Anyway," he continued, "you never answered my question."

"Oh, yeah," Derek replied, "Dave and his mom." He'd been so intent on his own move that for a moment he'd forgotten what his father had asked him. Now that it was brought back to his attention, he began shaking his head.

"You know how the Bulls can get—especially Brian," Derek explained to his father. "Brian's got us doing all these silly things for Mrs. Danzig. First we got her flowers. Then we washed her car. Last night we even cooked her dinner! Somehow Brian seems to think we're going to sweet-talk her out of this punishment."

Harold Roberts listened intently as his son talked. Then he said, "I know

Susan Danzig quite well. Your mom and I often sit with her in the bleachers during your games. She's pretty committed to Dave's punishment. There's no way she'd fall for that kind of stuff."

Derek waited patiently for his father to continue.

Mr. Roberts stroked his mustache thoughtfully, then added, "If you Bulls want to have a shot at changing her mind, you're going to have to lay off the brownnosing and try something a little more substantial."

"Okay, men, it's time to get going." The voice belonged to Mrs. Roberts, Derek's tall, attractive mother. She was calling out to Derek and his dad from the kitchen door, and Derek could see that she was ready to go. She already had on a long black coat with gold embroidered trim.

"And I heard what you two were talking about," Mrs. Roberts added. "I happen to know that what Susan Danzig is most concerned about is Dave's *grades*. If you Bulls could come up with something to get Dave back on track in school, I guarantee *that* would get Mrs. Danzig's attention."

Hmmm, Derek thought. *Maybe Mom's on to something there. . . .*

"Come on, grab your gym bag and let's head out," Mr. Roberts said. He rubbed his hands together. "We've got some serious butt to kick over in Essex."

"Let's not count our chickens before they're hatched," Derek countered, echoing Mr. Bowman's favorite expression. Nathaniel Bowman, Sr., Nate's dad, was the proprietor of Bowman's Market, where the Bulls gathered for sodas after every game and practice. Like the rest of the Bulls, Derek had tremendous affection for Mr. Bowman.

"We sometimes find weird ways to lose to sorry teams like Essex," Derek continued. "And besides, don't forget about Sky Jones. . . ."

CHAPTER 4

Derek stole a quick look up at the clock in the Essex Community Center gym. With three minutes and fifty-four seconds to go in the game, the Bulls were down

BULLS EAGLES
35 41

41–35. They hadn't led since early in the first quarter.

Derek's red jersey with the black number sixteen on it was drenched with sweat. Since the Eagles' coach hadn't rested Sky Jones even for a

31

minute, Jim and Nate had been afraid to remove their own star from the lineup. Derek knew he was the only one on the Bulls who could match up one-on-one against number thirty-seven, and he hadn't minded the extra playing time.

But now, more than halfway through the fourth quarter, he was having trouble catching his breath. He was also beginning to feel a painful stitch in his right side.

Sean McClain, the Eagles' point guard, brought the ball up the floor deliberately. Derek took advantage of the slow pace to lean over and try to get his wind back. But as soon as McClain passed the mid-court line, he gunned the ball over to Sky Jones.

So much for my rest period, Derek thought as he got back up on the balls of his feet.

Sky held the ball with two hands just off to his right, knees flexed, back bent at the waist. He was in the triple-threat position, ready to shoot, drive, or pass. *Knowing Sky,* Derek thought, *passing isn't a likely option.* While he and Sky were recognized as the two top players in the league, Sky was primarily a scorer. Derek was proud to be known as an all-around player.

He stayed in his defensive crouch. Against Sky Jones he had to be ready for anything. He didn't want to play right up in the Essex star's face, because then Sky could fry him with a sizzling move to the hoop. But if he gave him too much room, Jones would simply bury the open jumper.

Jones swung the ball from his right to his left, out in front of his body. Derek tried to stay balanced, ready to move in any direction. He had to admit that the sight of Sky with the ball was a scary one.

Jones was only about an inch taller than Derek, but he was a good deal more muscular than the Bulls' razor-thin forward. His black skin glistened with sweat under his neon orange-and-green uniform. The lightning bolt he had shaved in his hair only added to his intimidating appearance.

Finally Sky jerked the ball up high, as if he were shooting a jumper, but then took off to his right on a drive for the hoop.

Derek had anticipated the move, though, and he slid over to cut off Sky's path to the basket. Sky was forced to kick the ball out to Dee Francis in the right corner.

I'll take that any day, Derek thought, relieved the ball was out of Sky's hands.

But Francis, the Eagles' beanpole forward, took two dribbles closer to the basket, then drained the ten-footer.

Brian, who was supposed to be guarding Francis, was too slow getting to him to put on any real pressure.

Derek gave Brian a pained look. *Why do I seem to be the only one really working on defense?* Derek asked himself in frustration. *And why has Will done next to nothing all game? He and I can usually carry the whole team if we have to!*

Fortunately, Mark canned a fifteen-footer from left of the foul line on the Bulls' next trip downcourt. It

was Mark's first basket of the game. Though he'd been the hero the week before against Portsmouth, Derek knew it was asking too much of him to fill Dave's shoes for the entire game.

With the Bulls trailing 43–37, McClain again advanced the ball slowly for the Eagles—then suddenly accelerated, blowing by Jo for a layup. Derek actually felt kind of sorry for Jo. She was normally a tough defender, but with Dave out of the lineup, she'd played the entire game at point guard. Obviously it had taken a lot out of her. McClain had eaten her alive in the fourth quarter.

Derek knew he had to try to take over: It was now or never. And despite his exhaustion, he scored the Bulls' final six points and blocked two shots by Sky Jones. For the game, he'd outscored Sky fifteen to six.

On any normal day, Derek reflected, *you shut down Sky, and the Eagles are roadkill.*

But it wasn't a normal day. The Bulls' starting point guard was out of the lineup. And other than Derek himself, none of the other players seemed willing or able to pick up the slack. Even Will, probably the league's third-best player, had only five points—well below his average. The Bulls lost, 47–43.

The seven Bulls players milled around in front of the visitors' bench, waiting for a final word from the coaches. Derek knew from past experience that Nate would remain under control. But Jim, on the other hand . . . well, a blowup was not out of the question.

After a twenty-second silence Jim did address the players, but it wasn't with the fury Derek had anticipated. Actually, his voice was surprisingly quiet.

"Sure, you guys have won the March Madness contest," the coach said. "Congratulations. But you want to watch first place go down the tubes? Then just keep playing the way you played today."

Derek was waiting for him to say more, but Jim just grabbed his clipboard, the mesh ball bag, and his blue-and-white Branford varsity jacket. Then he headed for the exit.

Nate shrugged. "I've got nothing to add."

As the Bulls slowly followed their coaches, Will mumbled to Derek, "Mark and Jo played a good game, but there's nobody like Dave at the point. I don't know what we're going to do without him."

Derek nodded. He'd come to the same conclusion himself. With Dave missing, the whole team was out of sync.

If we don't find a way to get Mrs. Danzig to lift Dave's grounding, Derek thought, *the Bulls are going to self-destruct!*

CHAPTER 5

"How'd you guys do over the weekend?" Ms. Darling asked as Derek was placing a copy of *Maniac Magee* on each desk.

Derek grimaced. "We lost forty-seven to forty-three—to the Essex Eagles," he answered. He hated even thinking about it.

"Ouch!" Ms. Darling responded. "The Bulls lost to the *Eagles?* Don't they stink?"

Derek had to hand it to Ms. Darling. Most other teachers would have asked, "Aren't they kind of weak?" But Ms. Darling came right out with it. To Derek, everything about Ms. Darling was cool. She talked cool, she dressed cool—she even kept a poster of Dennis Rodman, with his green hair glowing, displayed on the wall behind her desk.

Every Monday after school Ms. Darling tutored students who were having trouble in reading, and Derek helped her. It wasn't something he'd ever told the Bulls about; they'd think it was geeky. But he *was* very good in English, and it made him feel good to be able to help other kids.

Besides, he thought Ms. Darling was really pretty.

Derek saw the teacher looking at him, and he realized he hadn't answered her question. "Yeah," he replied, "you're right, the Eagles *do* stink. But without Dave, I guess we're even worse."

"Oh, that's right, Dave's grounded.

I'd heard about that," Ms. Darling said with obvious concern.

That was another thing Derek liked about Ms. Darling. She didn't just teach; she also kept up with what was going on with the kids outside of school.

The first students began filing into the classroom. Derek recognized one of them, a slight, quiet boy with short, curly black hair named Alex Santos. He was in Derek's social studies class.

"Hey, Alex, what's up?" Ms. Darling asked with a warm smile. "We're going to get you up to that A range in English if it takes us all year, right?"

Alex smiled back and blushed.

Ms. Darling's greeting to Alex Santos switched a light bulb on in Derek's head.

What if we could boost Dave's grades up to the A range in English? Derek wondered. *Wouldn't that be the kind of substantial help Mom and Dad had said would catch Mrs. Danzig's attention?*

Derek allowed himself the slightest smile. *Forget Brian's so-called great ideas,* he thought. *Here's an idea that might finally get Mrs. Danzig to lift Dave's grounding once and for all!*

Derek balanced a dozen books against his chest and stomach as he hauled them back to the shelves. All the kids had left the classroom to wait out in front of the school for their rides home.

Only Derek and Ms. Darling remained.

"Man, you sure are good at teaching kids with reading problems," Derek ventured gingerly. He had an uncomfortable smile on his face.

Ms. Darling put her right hand on her hip and looked up at Derek. She was actually an inch or two shorter than he was.

"Okay, Derek," she said, "what is it you need from me? I can see the wheels spinning up there." She nodded at Derek's head.

How does she always know what I'm thinking? Derek wondered.

"Come on, out with it," the teacher prodded.

"Well, I was kind of thinking . . . about how you told Alex Santos you'd work with him to get his grade up to the A range," Derek said haltingly. "And, well, there's another kid I know who could use that kind of help. Only he wasn't here today."

Ms. Darling had her head tilted to one side, waiting. "And who might that be?"

Derek hesitated, then whispered, "Dave."

"Who?" Ms. Darling demanded.

"Dave Danzig," Derek repeated, this time in a huskier voice.

"That's what I thought you said," Ms. Darling answered. "Just wanted to make sure I heard you right. Are you trying to tell me Dave *wants* to do extra-credit work in English?"

"Well . . . not exactly," Derek admitted. "But he *needs* to!"

"Maybe *you* realize that and *I* realize that," the teacher said. "The fact is, though, I've already asked Dave to come in and work on an extra-credit paper."

"And?" Derek prompted.

"And he told me extra-credit papers are for dorks and kiss-ups," Ms. Darling replied.

Derek laughed and shook his head. "You know Dave," he said. "He always has to be Mr. Cool. But if I could get him to come in and work on an extra-credit paper, would you be willing to help him with it?"

Ms. Darling took a deep breath.

"I'll make you a deal," she said finally. "None of the Bulls, outside of you and Brian, is doing particularly well in English. Now, if you could bring the *whole team* in to work on extra-credit papers, I could help all the guys out—Dave especially."

Derek didn't respond. *All the Bulls*, he pondered. *Let's see. Maybe—*

"But to tell you the truth," Ms. Darling continued, interrupting his train of thought, "I don't think you can pull it off. When Dave says he thinks extra-credit papers are for losers, I'm pretty sure he speaks for the rest of the team."

Derek scratched his head. His forehead was furrowed in concentration.

"Ms. Darling," he blurted out all of a sudden, "do you think the Bulls could work on these papers someplace outside your classroom?"

Ms. Darling shrugged. "We could do this session on the *moon* for all I care, as long as I have everybody's attention." Noticing Derek's mysterious smile, she added, "Why, Derek? What are you thinking?"

"I'll work out the details, Ms. Darling," Derek said, his mood brightening. "Just leave it to me."

CHAPTER 6

"Come on, who's it going to be? Larry Bird?" Mark wanted to know. "Please, please, *please* tell us," he begged, pulling on the sleeve of Derek's ski jacket. Although Mark was doing his pretend spoiled-little-brat act, Derek knew he really *did* want to know who was waiting at Derek's house. All the Bulls wanted to know.

"I told you, it's not *that* kind of mystery guest," Derek said, trying to sound convincing.

"I'll bet it's Isiah Thomas," Will volunteered. "Mr. Roberts always talks about how he used to be like *this* with most of the Pistons." He held up his right hand, with the index and middle fingers crossed over each other.

It was Wednesday afternoon, and all the Bulls—minus Jo, who lived in Sampton, not Branford, and went to a different school—were tromping over to Derek's house straight from Benjamin Franklin Middle School. Their spirits were sky-high.

Ever since the previous summer, when Derek had introduced the Bulls to his dad, Hall of Fame center Harold "Rebound" Roberts, they'd been on the lookout for Mr. Roberts's famous NBA buddies. As soon as he'd let the words *mystery guest* out of his mouth, Derek knew he'd made a big mistake.

"No, it's not Isiah Thomas," Derek said to Will. "It's not that kind of mystery guest," he insisted for about the tenth time.

"Magic Johnson!" Brian shouted. "It's going to be Magic Johnson!"

Derek just shook his head.

As they turned the last corner and the Robertses' house and wide driveway came into view, Dave called out, "Is that *Ms. Darling* I see?"

It sure is, Derek thought, wondering anxiously how his teammates would react. He noticed that Ms. Darling was wearing a bulky purple parka over tight black leggings and had a black plastic whistle on a lanyard around her neck.

And she was dribbling a basketball. Well, not exactly *dribbling* it, but slapping at it with two hands, the way a three-year-old would. Derek remembered her unique style of dribbling from when the Bulls had played the Benjamin Franklin Middle School faculty the previous fall.

"Hey, Ms. Darling," Will called out. "What's up? You here to meet Derek's mystery guest too?"

Derek gulped.

"Uh, g-guys," he finally stammered. All eyes were on him. "Ms. Darling *is* the mystery guest. That's what I've been trying to explain the whole way over here."

"Yeah, right!" Dave scoffed. "Come on, Derek, you can stop playing games with us. We want to meet Bird . . . or Thomas . . . or Johnson . . . or *whoever* it is."

"Guys, *listen*," Derek said, still softly, but with a little more force. "I asked Ms. Darling to come over and help us with some extra-credit papers." He felt a little breathless. He wasn't used to addressing the whole team. But he plunged on. "No one here is doing all that great. Especially Dave. If we don't help him get his grades up . . . no Final Four!"

Derek could see by the Bulls' faces that they were stunned. And angry.

"How could you bring us over here and make us think we're going to meet someone *important*," Will asked, "and then it turns out to be Ms. Darling?" Will looked over at the teacher, then added with a nervous laugh, "No offense, Ms. Darling."

"And who gave you the right to agree we'd do extra-credit papers without our say-so?" Brian added.

"Besides," Dave chimed in with a sneer, "since when do the Bulls do kiss-up extra-credit work? What would the kids at school think?"

While his teammates were whining, Derek saw Ms. Darling step to the white free-throw line that Mr. Roberts had painted on the driveway. She shot the ball underhand, from between her legs, the way the old-timers did. It landed with a thud on the asphalt, several feet short of the hoop.

"Ms. Darling," Dave said with a snort, "that was one ugly shot!"

"Oh, yeah?" Ms. Darling challenged. "Describe it."

"Well, you—"

"No, no, Dave," Ms. Darling cut him off. "Describe it on paper. In the garage. I've set up a table with lots of paper and pencils. Now go on and get busy."

Ms. Darling's tone of voice left no room for argument. Derek saw Dave resignedly slouch into the garage.

"Since my shot was so ugly, as Dave very nicely put it, I want you all to watch Derek shoot a free throw," Ms. Darling commanded.

Derek bent over to pick up the ball, which had rolled off onto the snow-covered grass alongside the driveway. He felt a little self-conscious with all the Bulls staring at him. Still, everything about his shot—from the grip to the release and the follow-through—was perfect. The ball swished cleanly

through the net without even grazing the rim.

"Hey, that was pretty nice," Ms. Darling said admiringly. "Now, everyone hustle into the garage, pick up a pencil and paper, and describe Derek's shot—in detail."

Derek heard a few groans go up from his teammates.

"As a matter of fact, why don't you compare Derek's form to mine?" Ms. Darling added. "Come on, I can take it."

Despite the grumbling, the Bulls settled down to work. *Perfect!* Derek thought. He'd known when he hatched his plan that Ms. Darling would find a way to get what she wanted out of the Bulls.

"Dave, let's hear yours first," Ms. Darling commanded after all the pencils had stopped moving.

Dave stood up, tossed his blond hair out of his eyes, and cleared his throat. "You asked for it," he warned.

Ms. Darling just nodded.

"Okay," Dave said. "'Wearing her big

purple parka and her skinny black tights, and shooting the ball underhand,'" he read, "'Ms. Darling looked kind of like an ostrich hatching an egg.'"

Derek wasn't sure how Ms. Darling would react.

But after a split second's silence she laughed out loud and said, "Dave, that's *perfect*. What a vivid picture you painted! Now tell us how my shot compared to Derek's."

Derek saw Dave's face flush a little as he looked at his paper. "'Though Ms. Darling is a lot prettier than Derek,'" Dave read, "'Derek's shot is a lot prettier than Ms. Darling's.'"

This time all the Bulls laughed, along with Ms. Darling.

"Flattery will get you everywhere," the teacher said to Dave with a smile. Then she added in a confidential tone, "You know, Dave, you could be quite a writer if you wanted to be."

Ms. Darling next had the Bulls run their favorite weave drill. Then she asked them to sit down and describe in writing how the drill felt. Though there were still a few objections, Derek could tell the Bulls were starting to enjoy the session.

Fifteen minutes later Ms. Darling had the boys wrapped around her finger. Derek knew how much all the guys on the team liked Ms. Darling, and he'd gambled that she'd be able to win them over.

The Bulls were involved in a heated game of knockout when Ms. Darling blew her whistle.

"Okay, guys, here's what we're going to do now," the teacher said as the boys gathered around her. "This will be our last exercise of the day."

"'Bout time," Will said, but he was grinning as he spoke.

"I want you to think about the most important basketball game you ever played," Ms. Darling continued. "Then I want you to write what you remember about the game, including why it was so important to you. Write at least a page."

"A page!" Mark squawked. "That'll take forever!"

"Take all the time you need," Ms. Darling explained calmly. "This will serve as your extra-credit paper. If it's good, you can count it for twenty percent of your grade for the quarter. If it's not good, it won't count at all."

Derek thought the offer sounded more than fair. Dave moaned and groaned, as usual, about not wanting to get involved in this brownnose stuff. Eventually, though, he settled down to write, just like the rest of the Bulls.

Thirty minutes later all the papers had been turned in—except Dave's. He was still complaining loudly, but Derek noticed he'd done a lot of writing—more than three pages' worth. The title of Dave's composition, Derek could see, was "Above the Rim."

Finally Dave got up from the table

and handed his paper to Ms. Darling. "Just make sure you give me an A-plus on this," he said with a snicker, for the benefit of his teammates. "Another D, like the one I got on the *Old Yeller* test, and I'll be grounded for a year!"

Ms. Darling told the Bulls she'd enjoyed the session, thanked them for their hard work, and promised she'd have their papers back to them by Friday.

"I'll walk you to your car," Derek offered politely.

Out of earshot of the rest of the Bulls, Ms. Darling said to Derek, "Brilliant! Your plan worked like a charm." She had a wide smile on her face.

Derek looked down at the tops of his sneakers. "Couldn't have done it without you," he mumbled.

Then they exchanged a low five before she got in her car and drove away.

CHAPTER 7

Derek peeked at the plain round clock on the wall of the classroom. It was 2:05. Last time he'd checked it had been 2:02. Why did the period seem to be dragging on forever?

Derek, Will, Brian, and Dave were all in Ms. Darling's last-period English class together. And it was Friday—the day she'd promised to return the extra-credit papers they'd done at his house two days earlier.

But so far she hadn't said a word about them.

Derek could see he wasn't the only

one feeling a little edgy. Though Dave was goofing around as usual, Derek noticed he was also continually drumming his fingers nervously on his desk and constantly looking up at the clock.

At 2:20 Ms. Darling told the class they could put away their books.

Finally, Derek thought.

"I have some extra-credit papers I'd like to hand back and go over," the teacher announced. "Jordan, would you mind coming up and getting yours first?"

Derek saw Brian and Dave snickering. Jordan Resnick, a tall girl with a long brown ponytail, was the most notorious brownnoser in the class. She turned in extra-credit papers just about every week. Derek and the rest of the Bulls always found her topics extremely corny.

Jordan passed Derek's desk on the way back to her seat. Derek could see she'd gotten an A-minus.

Ms. Darling asked her to read her

essay to the class, and, as always, Jordan was happy to comply. She'd written about how her relatives from all over the country had gotten together in Branford for her grandmother's seventy-fifth birthday. Her final sentence was, "I only hope Grandma Rose lives to be a hundred, so that we can all get together again."

Brian and Dave guffawed but were silenced by a threatening look from Ms. Darling.

A short, wiry boy named Alexander Petropoulis was next. His composition was about his coin-collecting hobby and a coveted rare coin he'd received as a gift from his parents.

Then Ms. Darling called on Will Hopwood.

"*Will Hopwood?*" Jordan Resnick piped up. "I thought the Bulls *never* did extra-credit papers!" Derek knew she was trying to pay his teammates back for all the grief they always gave her about brownnosing.

"Yes, actually, a few of the Bulls

have done extra-credit papers this time around," Ms. Darling responded, trying to make light of the issue. "I asked them to write about the most important basketball game they'd ever played. And they all did a pretty nice job. Will?" she asked, motioning him to come forward.

Will walked up to get his essay from Ms. Darling. As he returned to his seat he responded to the questioning looks from his teammates by mouthing, "B-plus."

At Ms. Darling's request, he read his composition to the class. It was about a Bulls' victory over the Portsmouth Panthers the summer before—the game after he and Brian had made up following a huge fight.

After Will's reading, Brian and Derek got their papers back. Brian, who'd written about the Bulls' come-from-behind triumph over the Sampton Slashers when Mr. Bowman returned from his heart attack, got an A-minus. Derek's composition was about the first game he played after making the Bulls, when he was new in town. He got an A, as usual.

As Derek read his essay to the class, he felt an uncomfortable dryness in his throat that made it difficult for him to speak above a whisper. He *hated* to share his private feelings. He noticed, however, that he wasn't the only one who was suffering. Dave was squirming in his chair. He couldn't seem to sit still at all.

"Ms. Darling," Dave finally blurted out when Derek had finished reading. The normal coolness was gone from his voice. "What happened to *my* paper? We've heard everyone else's. Was mine really so bad?"

Ms. Darling made a big show of fumbling around in her briefcase. Several seconds went by before she pulled his paper out. With a stern look on her face, she handed it to him—facedown.

All the Bulls waited for him to turn it over.

Finally, with a no-big-deal shrug, he flipped over the pages so he could see his grade.

Derek saw Dave's face turn bright red. "Well?" Derek asked impatiently.

For a long time Dave couldn't seem to speak. "A-plus," he finally whispered.

"Would you read it, Dave?" Ms. Darling asked. "I know it's very personal, but I'd love for you to share it with the class."

Dave nodded. In a hushed voice—far from his normal wise-guy tone—he read about a game the Bulls had played against the Winsted Wildcats a few seasons back. The seriousness of his story, coupled with the unusual solemnity of his voice, had the class sitting totally still.

"'It wasn't a championship game,'" Dave read, drawing toward the conclusion.

"'And it wasn't even a game that I played all that great. But it was a very special game for me, because it's the last game my dad saw me play before he died.'"

Nobody moved. Nobody talked.

"Dave, that was amazing," Ms. Darling said finally. "Absolutely *amazing*. I just have one question for you. Why did you call it 'Above the Rim'?"

"When I play now," Derek heard his friend answer, his voice quivering, "that's where I know my dad's watching from."

Brian, knowing that Mrs. Danzig could hear their conversation as she did the dinner dishes, said, "Can you believe that A-plus Dave got on his English composition today? I mean, is that improvement, or what?"

Will, picking up on the cue, said, "Forget the A-plus. How 'bout those comments Ms. Darling wrote on his paper? Stuff about 'tremendous effort' and 'finally starting to reach his potential.' And didn't she say his classroom participation is getting better all the time?"

"Too bad he's still not allowed to play with us tomorrow against the Hornets," Brian pursued. "We sure could use him. We just don't seem to be the same team without him."

Laying it on a little thick, aren't they? Derek thought. He took a quick look at Mrs. Danzig to see what effect their conversation was having on her. He was worried that after the flowers, the car wash, and the dinner, this hard-sell stuff wasn't going to work well with her at all.

Much to his surprise, however, he saw a smile on Mrs. Danzig's face.

"Yes, I can hear what you boys are saying," she acknowledged, "and you're absolutely right. Dave *has* made a lot of progress with his schoolwork."

Derek couldn't believe it. Were all their efforts finally starting to pay off?

"I should also add," Mrs. Danzig continued, "that when I grounded Dave, it was never my intention to penalize the whole team for my son's behavior. I didn't mean for you to lose games—or to ruin your team trip to Indianapolis for the Final Four."

Derek waited, holding his breath. *What is she driving at?*

"What I'm going to do," Mrs. Danzig said finally, "is lift Dave's grounding *temporarily*—just for tomorrow's game against Harrison. After that . . . we'll see."

Derek felt breathless. His plan—far-fetched as it had appeared—actually seemed to be working!

He pumped his arm in victory. *Yes!*

CHAPTER 8

Derek knew that Mike Van Siclen was dying to block his shot. All game long Derek had been burning the Hornets' tall, stringy forward with jumpers. Now Van Siclen was looking for payback time. Derek could see it in his eyes.

Derek threw a quick pump fake, and Van Siclen fell for it. As soon as the Hornets' forward left his feet, Derek drove around him for an easy hoop.

The Bulls led 29–23. Five minutes remained in the third quarter.

"Smooth move, Genius," Brian called out with a smile, offering Derek his hand for a low five.

Brian had been calling Derek "Genius" since the previous evening, when, thanks to Derek's extra-credit paper scheme, Mrs. Danzig had temporarily lifted Dave's grounding. Derek could tell Brian was slightly resentful that it was Derek's plan that had worked, after all of his own "great ideas" had gone up in smoke.

On the whole, though, Brian and all the rest of the Bulls were elated to have Dave back. Derek could see it in the way they played.

The Bulls had entered the game with a six-and-two record, with Harrison right behind at five and three. And despite constant pressure from the Hornets, an excellent defensive team, the Bulls had maintained a four- to six-point lead throughout. Dave, far from being rusty after his two-week layoff, was having his best game of the season.

Derek felt pretty pleased with himself for his part in bringing Dave back to the team. And he also liked what he saw up in the bleachers.

Ms. Darling had come to Harrison to see the game and was sitting with his parents and Mrs. Danzig. Derek saw a lot of laughing and backslapping going on. Though, of course, he wasn't able to hear what they were saying, the big smiles couldn't be a bad sign.

But while his teammates were acting as if their problem were solved for good, Derek kept hearing the echo of what Dave's mother had said the night before: *I'm lifting Dave's grounding* temporarily—*just for tomorrow's game against Harrison. After that . . . we'll see.*

Derek realized Dave had passed one of Mrs. Danzig's tests: He'd picked up his grades in school. Now she wanted to see how he'd behave on the basketball court. And Derek knew the Hornets had a couple of players who could test anyone's temper.

With three minutes left in the quarter and the Bulls holding on to a 34–29

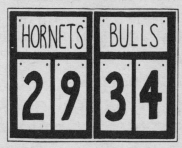

lead, Dave tried to snake through the lane. He'd been having a lot of success drawing defenders to him and then dishing off to open teammates.

This time, as Dave motored past the foul line, Elvis Bailey, the Hornets' tall, meaty center, stuck his leg out and sent Dave sprawling. The ref didn't see Bailey's dirty move, so no foul was called.

Derek noticed Bailey smirking at

Dave through his braces. And he heard Devon Haskins, Harrison's show-off point guard, whisper to Dave, "Stay out of the lane, blondie. It's no place for skinny little mama's boys like you."

All the Hornets knew Dave had a short fuse. Derek realized they were trying to get him to explode. He saw Dave on the hardwood floor, his fists clenched.

Not now, Derek prayed. *Not now. Think about Indianapolis. Think about the Final Four.*

But to Derek's surprise, Dave simply picked himself off the floor, checked his right ankle for damage, and, when he saw everything was okay, got ready to play again.

Derek finally exhaled. He hadn't even realized he'd been holding his breath.

Throughout the rest of the period, and midway into the fourth quarter, the Bulls held on to their modest lead.

With his team ahead 42–38, Dave dribbled hard to the foul line and looked as though he was going to continue on to the hoop. Suddenly, however, he put on the brakes and pulled up for a jumper.

Devon Haskins, an excellent defender, had stayed right with him, stride for stride. But in trying to block his shot, he poked Dave in the right eye.

The ref immediately called Haskins for the foul, sending Dave to the line. Though to Derek the poke looked completely accidental, he could see that Dave was furious. Since Haskins had been taunting him earlier, Dave seemed sure that the Hornets' guard was out to get him.

Haskins moved toward mid-court, his normal position when an opposing player was shooting free throws. But Dave, instead of heading for the foul line, began stalking Devon Haskins.

Here it goes, Derek thought. *Everything we've accomplished, down the drain!*

Instinctively Derek stepped between Dave and Devon Haskins. He didn't grab his teammate or restrain him in any way; he knew Dave would flip out if he did that. He simply whispered, "Final Four, Dave. Final Four."

Dave looked Derek in the eye. Derek saw his mouth turn up in the slightest hint of a smile. Dave didn't say a word, but suddenly the anger drained from his face. He turned his back on Haskins, stepped to the free-throw line, and calmly made both his shots.

The Bulls led 44–38.

For the second time that game Derek allowed himself a big sigh of relief. He looked up at the bleachers and saw Mrs. Danzig beaming. Next to her was Ms. Darling, giving him a thumbs-up.

The Bulls outscored the Hornets 9–2 over the final three and a half minutes. Derek and Dave each had two baskets; Will added a free throw.

The Bulls won 53–40, tightening their hold on first place.

The Bulls and Hornets had finished shaking hands. Now the parents, who had made their way down the bleacher steps, were congratulating the kids and the coaches.

When Dave spotted his mother, he began apologizing before she could even say a word.

"I'm sorry, Mom. I know I shouldn't have gone after Haskins. That's exactly what you warned me about. It's just that—"

"Dave, Dave," Mrs. Danzig broke in, cutting him off in midsentence. "I was *thrilled* by what I saw today. I know what was going on out there. I saw that boy egging you on—and yet you were smart enough to walk away from it."

Dave glanced over at Derek and gave him a quick, secret wink. Derek was glad Dave appreciated his part in all this.

"Ms. Darling's been going on and on all game about what you've accomplished in the classroom," Mrs. Danzig continued, "and about how Derek got you to do that extra-credit paper." She turned and looked at Derek. "I can't tell you how much I appreciate what you did for Dave."

No one spoke. Derek felt his cheeks burning.

Brian broke the awkward silence. "Mrs. Danzig," he ventured, "you think you might keep Dave's grounding lifted through next Saturday? We play Torrington, and we could sure use Dave for that one."

"I'll do better than that, Brian," Mrs. Danzig said, a gleam in her blue eyes.

Derek felt his heart pounding. *Could it be true?*

"Dave's grounding is lifted—for good!" Mrs. Danzig said.

"All right!" the Bulls yelled together. They danced around Mrs. Danzig, punching the air with their fists.

"Hey, Mrs. D., why don't you come along with us to Indianapolis?" Brian suggested. "Contest rules say we have to bring some parents along."

Derek wasn't at all surprised by Brian's invitation. He'd always suspected that Brian had a little bit of a crush on Mrs. Danzig.

"Funny you should ask," Mrs.

Danzig replied. "That's just what we were talking about in the bleachers. Turns out I'm going to join Mr. and Mrs. Roberts as your chaperons. Indianapolis, here we come!"

Derek had had his fair share of excitement since joining the Bulls. He'd been their high scorer more times than he could remember, and he'd won games with clutch shots at the buzzer once or twice.

But he'd never felt as proud as he felt at that moment.

CHAPTER 9

"Now, gentlemen, don't get carried away," Mr. Roberts cautioned as the Bulls filed down to their plush court-side seats at the RCA Dome. "You *are* representing the town of Branford and the Danville County Basketball League."

Derek was neither surprised nor embarrassed to hear his dad's warning. Mr. Roberts was from the old school, but Derek never minded the discipline. He sure couldn't complain about the way he was brought up. How many other kids had three former members of the Pistons over to their house for Thanksgiving dinner, the way his own family had the year before?

Derek turned around and looked at the upper tiers of the arena. Thousands and thousands of people! It was still forty-five minutes to tip-off, and most of the seats were already filled. The noise level was cranked up so high he could barely hear his teammates' conversation.

Not exactly like when the Branford Bulls play in the Clifton Community Center or the gym in Portsmouth, Derek thought.

Chunky settled into one of the luxury seats and made himself comfortable. "Now this is what I've been waiting for," the Bulls' pale backup center said with satisfaction. "We can *touch* the players from here!"

Derek knew exactly what Chunky was talking about. This was the big Saturday doubleheader—two semifinal games, back-to-back. A lot of people would prefer tickets to this attraction than to the Monday night final, if they had to choose.

Fortunately, the Bulls didn't have to choose. They'd be there for *both*.

"You're just glad 'cause you're finally out of the Bullsmobile," Dave commented.

Chunky had made *everybody* aware that he'd been carsick for the entire four-hour drive from Branford, Illinois, to Indianapolis, Indiana. Though Nate had gone easy on the gas pedal, with Mr. and Mrs. Roberts and Mrs. Danzig trailing them in the Robertses' car, it hadn't helped Chunky. He always got sick pretty much the moment he set foot in a car.

While the Bulls chattered on excitedly, a slender, well-dressed African

American man of about six foot three came around behind Mr. Roberts and jabbed him in the ribs. "Rebound!" he shouted. "Long time no see!" The newcomer had sparkling, wide-set eyes, a handsome face, and a grin that could light up the arena.

Before Mr. Roberts could even respond, Derek recognized the man as one of his dad's best friends from his NBA days.

Derek wasn't the only one who recognized the former guard. A huge knot of kids had scurried from their seats with their pens and autograph pads and were now crowding the celebrities. *If these kids were packed in any tighter*, Derek thought, *they'd be sitting on my lap!*

"Joe!" Mr. Roberts shouted with glee. "Great to see you!"

The two men hugged each other. To Derek, it almost looked like father and son, since his dad was a full head taller than the former star guard.

"Joe, you remember my wife,

Beverly?" Mr. Roberts said, his hand on Mrs. Roberts's shoulder. "And my son, Derek? And these are Derek's teammates on the Branford Bulls, and his coaches, Jim and Nate. The Bulls are the first-place team in the Danville County Basketball League."

"Oh, so *this* is the team that won the March Madness contest," Joe said with an appreciative smile. "I'd heard about that."

"That's us!" Dave said, thumping his chest proudly.

Derek couldn't believe the former NBA great had heard about the March Madness contest. He had a hard time controlling his smile.

"Now, who are the guards on this team?" Mr. Roberts' friend asked.

"That would be me," Dave answered without hesitation.

"Me too," Jo piped up.

"Me three," Mark added.

"Well, I'd like to talk to you guys, guard to guard," Joe said, looking at Mr. Roberts with a knowing grin.

"But I know deep down you probably think of me as an old-timer, like Mr. Roberts. So I brought along one of my buddies, someone you might relate to a little more."

Derek could hardly believe his eyes. Strolling toward them, straight from a TV interview he'd just finished, was one of the top college guards in the

country! Derek had known that he and his teammates might get to meet some of the big names from his dad's generation, but he had no idea they'd be meeting current stars too!

Again the kids from the neighboring sections rushed in for autographs, but this time a huge security guard stepped in and sent them back to their seats.

While Derek was still reeling from

the thrill of meeting the All-America playmaker, he heard another man's booming voice.

"Yo, Rebound, what's up?"

Derek looked to see who was connected to the voice. He spotted a tall, pale man with light brown hair and a brown mustache.

"Cliff Warwick," Derek murmured in awe.

"Hey, Cliff, what are *you* doing here?" Mr. Roberts asked, clapping the former NBA All-Star on the back.

"Well, my hometown is only about a two-hour drive from here," the tall forward replied, "and I thought I'd come around and see how these young guys measure up." He gestured in the direction of the players on the two teams warming up for the semifinal matchup.

Mark walked up right in front of Mr. Roberts's friend. His eyes were level with the superstar's belly button.

"So close I can touch him," Mark murmured, shaking his head in disbelief. "You used to be my favorite player!"

"*Used* to be?" Cliff replied, pretending his feelings were hurt. "And who's your favorite player now?"

"Allen Iverson," Mark admitted sheepishly. "No offense . . ."

Derek noticed a tall, skinny, black-haired man with a mike approaching the group.

"Oh, baby, are these the Branford Bulls?" the man asked in a high-pitched, bubbling voice. "This is great. I'm going to get you guys on TV in just a minute." Then, putting his hands on Derek's shoulders, he said, "I hear this kid can really take it to the hole!"

"I've seen him on TV," Will whispered in wonderment. "And he's going to interview *us!*" Will slapped himself on the head.

As Will was talking, a stray ball hit Brian on the knee.

"Yo, you with the fade haircut," one of the college hotshots called out. "Wanna send that back over here?"

Brian obediently threw the player a sharp bounce pass.

"Brian, you look like you just went to heaven!" Jo observed.

Derek tried to take it all in. The former NBA greats, the NCAA stars, being interviewed on national TV, the courtside seats . . . he just kept shaking his head. "I can't believe this," he said to Dave, who was standing next to him. "I just can't believe it. It's like a dream."

"You got that right," Dave agreed solemnly. Then, looking at Derek, he added, "And if it weren't for you, I would have missed it!"

"This place definitely beats McDonald's!" MJ said, his eyes taking in all the NBA memorabilia on the walls of the restaurant.

All the Bulls had wanted fast food, of course, for their final meal in Indianapolis, but Mr. Roberts had steered them to a restaurant that he knew was a Pacers hangout.

Sure enough, Derek and his friends had already spotted Reggie Miller, Rik Smits, and Dale Davis—and the Bulls were only up to their appetizers!

As the waiter distributed the sodas from his tray, Mr. Roberts raised his glass and proposed a toast. "To our Branford

Bulls," he said proudly, "Danville County Basketball League champs!"

Mrs. Danzig clinked his glass with her own. "I'll drink to that—and I have something a little mushier to add. I hope I won't embarrass anybody."

Derek knew what was coming, and he already felt his face flushing.

"You all know that Dave almost didn't make it on this amazing trip," Mrs.

Danzig began. "And if I had kept him home as I threatened, he would have been pretty impossible to live with."

"You can say that again!" Dave chimed in.

Everyone laughed.

"But thanks to all you Bulls," Mrs. Danzig continued, "and *especially* to Derek, everything worked out for the best."

Derek looked down at his glass. He was too uncomfortable to look Dave's mother in the eye. He hated to be in the spotlight.

"Anyway," Mrs. Danzig said, "you guys are the greatest!"

Dave stood up and threw his arm around his mother's shoulder. Derek was expecting a wisecrack, but Dave just said, "As moms go, you're not so bad yourself."

Mrs. Danzig beamed. Then a puzzled expression crossed her face. She looked straight at Derek.

"I was just wondering, Derek," she began. "After all those stunts you guys pulled—the flowers, the car wash, the dinner—how'd you know that boosting up Dave's grades was going to make me lift his grounding?"

Derek shot his mother and father a sly grin.

"Oh," he answered with a shrug, "just a lucky guess."

Don't miss Super Hoops #12,
In the Zone. Coming soon!

Brian instantly drove around the off-balance coach and scored the easy layup.

"Way to toast him!" Dave crowed.

"But use your left next time," MJ couldn't keep himself from adding.

Brian shot MJ a deadly look. "*What?*" he demanded.

"You took the layup with your right hand," MJ explained matter-of-factly. "You should use your left hand when you drive to the left. Especially in practice, when it doesn't really matter if you miss. The coaches always tell us that."

The more MJ spoke, the more self-conscious he felt. He noticed the whole team had gotten very, very quiet.

Brian slowly ran his hand through his fade haircut, taking his time to reply.

"*You're* trying to tell *me* to use my left hand?" he asked finally, in a menacing tone. "At least I *made* the layup. You couldn't make a layup with your *right* hand—if your life depended on it!"

About the Author

Hank Herman is a writer and newspaper columnist who lives in Connecticut with his wife, Carol, and their three sons, Matt, Greg, and Robby.

His column, "The Home Team," appears in the *Westport News*. It's about kids, sports, and life in the suburbs.

Although Mr. Herman was formerly the editor in chief of *Health* magazine, he now writes mostly about sports. At one time, he was a tennis teacher, and he has also run the New York City Marathon. He coaches kids' basketball every winter and Little League baseball every spring.

He runs, bicycles, skis, kayaks, and plays tennis and basketball on a regular basis. Mr. Herman admits that he probably spends about as much time playing, coaching, and following sports as he does writing.

Of all sports, basketball is his favorite.